THE SOLD SOULS

THE SOLD SOULS

THE SOLD SOULS

Edgar J. Hyde

© 1997 Children's Choice Publications Ltd

Text supplied by Alan J. H. Keenan

All rights reserved. No part of this publication may be
reproduced, stored in a retrieval system, or transmitted, in any
form or by any means, electronic, mechanical, photocopying,
recording or otherwise without the prior permission of the
copyright holder.

ISBN 1 902012 03 2

Printed and bound in UK

CCP

© 1997 Children's Choice Publications Ltd

Text supplied by Alan J. Henderson

ISBN 1 90201 203 8

Printed and bound in UK

Contents

Contents

Chapter 1

Steve smirked and looked at his companions. Then, turning to me he said, "So you want to be one of us then, Ben."

I was trembling inside but looked him straight in the eye and said, "Yea, I've got what it takes to be one of you guys."

These guys were the tops in this school. Steve along with Emma, Chip and Sam were the "A-Team". They could run faster, think smarter, look better and had everything money could buy compared to anyone else. I was desperate to be one of them.

Of course, they could be arrogant and cruel, but I just accepted that was a part of being the elite. I wanted to feel superior just like they did. They were all filled with ambitions to be the best and I had to have the same.

The leader was Steve, he was the biggest and best athlete in our school. The boys all admired his feats, and the girls flocked around him. Although not as intelligent as Chip, or dare I say, myself, he had a natural air of authority about him. When he spoke you listened.

Emma was Steve's girlfriend. She was beautiful and she knew it. Fashion was her obsession and she wanted to be a model after leaving school. It would be too easy to look upon her as an "air-head". She was very bright and filled with a steely ambition that would get where she wanted to go.

The other girl in this elite group was Sam. Again, she was intelligent and attractive. Her goal was to make it in TV and films. Sam could be loud and emotional at times, but everybody had an admiration for her.

Chip was the fourth member of the elite, which I hoped, with me as the new addition, would become five. Douglas was his real name, but because of his love of all things connected with computing he was given the name "Chip". With large black rimmed spectacles, a long nose and a lanky body, he was hardly what you would call handsome. However, he was the most intelligent person I had ever come across. You couldn't tell him anything – he already knew.

"Well, to join us you'll have to go through

our little initiation ceremony," said Steve. The others looked at him slightly puzzled. Steve had obviously thought of this by himself.

I replied, "Sure, whatever it takes. I can handle it."

Steve beckoned to the others to join him in a private conversation. I felt a bit awkward but kept up my look of confidence. There were a few giggles from them, but I tried not to let them annoy me.

Emma came forward and said, "I'll let you into a little secret of ours. How do you think we have managed to gain the position of top dogs around here?"

I shrugged my shoulders and replied, "Don't know."

Slowly a smile came over Emma's face and she continued, "We have some help from him down below."

I thought this over for a few moments and repeated, "Down below," without understanding what she meant.

"Yes, him down below, the Devil," she said.

I thought she was joking and laughed, "Oh, yea."

Chip entered the conversation and added, "Who do you think we mean – the janitor!"

Were they being serious? I thought to myself as I swallowed hard. They are an ambitious bunch, but, would they go to that length to achieve success? I wondered. I decided then to play along and see what happened next.

"Are you still interested, Ben?" said Sam. She looked deadly serious as she asked me.

I raised a smile and assured them, "Yes, of course. I want to be one of you guys."

"Right, here's what we're going to do. We'll meet at the old church behind Main Street tonight at nine o'clock. Don't tell anyone what we are up to or else you're out. Okay?" said Steve.

"Okay," I replied, not knowing what to expect.

Chapter 2

It was a cold, clear autumn night. By nine o'clock it had been dark for a few hours. Steve and Emma were waiting outside for me.

"Are you ready for this?" asked Emma.

"As ready as I'll ever be," I replied.

They smiled at each other with an air of superiority that I wished I had.

"Where are Sam and Chip?" I enquired. I was told they were inside making preparations for my initiation. I assumed this meant candles and torches as the building had no power.

The old church had been abandoned years ago. It was supposed to be boarded up, but if you went round the back and climbed onto a ledge you could squeeze behind a loose board and then through a window. We were the only ones who knew about this way in.

Once inside it was like an empty shell. Most of the fittings and pews had been removed, but you could see from the roof, pillars and carvings that it had once been a church. The roof was still water-tight and the inside was dry and dusty.

Sam and Chip were on the raised platform where the altar once stood. They had brought lots of candles and arranged them in a circle. For effect one of them had brought a sheep's skull and a chalice. The chalice was full of what appeared to be blood. I was shocked for a moment until I sniffed and recognised the sour but sweet smell of tomato ketchup.

Sam remarked, "Ah, our next victim." The others laughed and I gave a timid smile.

To my surprise, they each proceeded to adorn themselves in what appeared to be red satin robes. I detected a few sniggers and gained the impression they were not as serious as they had made out. This, at least, made me feel a bit more relaxed.

Emma gave me a white robe and told me to put it on. I felt silly but went along with her instructions. Chip could hardly stifle a laugh at this point, and I was further convinced that it was all a set up for their amusement. But, I thought, if I've come this far I may as well continue with their little game.

"Are we ready to proceed, brothers and sisters?" Steve announced in a formal tone. They each nodded in turn.

"Are you ready to proceed?" asked Steve to me.

"Yes," I replied, trying not to giggle.

Steve beckoned me to stand in the middle of the circle of candles. They stood outside the circle as if at the corners of a square with me in the centre.

Chip then began chanting something which sounded like Latin. I figured the others had left this to him as he had more than enough brain power to master that old language. To my surprise the others joined in at certain points. Although I wasn't really taking the ceremony seriously, I suppose it appeared like quite an impressive fake.

The chanting stopped. "Lord of Darkness, I awake thee," Steve suddenly chanted in a loud voice. "We offer our souls for thy assistance, and offer a new soul from Ben," Steve cried. "Please accept this offer and allow him to become one of us," he continued.

Steve then stopped as if thinking what to say next. After a moments silence the temperature around us suddenly plunged. We all shivered and looked at one another in puzzlement. Then an icy blast of wind from nowhere blew all the candles out. Sam and Emma screamed. The rest of us where rooted to the spot in terror.

Beside the circle, where the pulpit used to be, appeared a small figure bathed in a mysterious red light. There was a foul stench of sulphur in the air. I couldn't believe what I was seeing.

Chapter 3

"What's going on?" I asked the others. They stood frozen in fear unable to speak.

I tried to joke, "Hey, this is really impressive, where is the projector hidden?"

Chip spoke quietly, "This is no joke – this is really happening."

Before us stood a small demonic figure with gargoyle-like features, pointed tail, wings and talons for its hands and feet. It sat there looking at us with an evil grin on its face for a short while.

Then it asked, "Why do you wish to summon my master?"

Steve managed to mumble out, "Are you for real?"

"Of course I am, do you not believe your eyes?" the figure responded. "You may call me Moloch. I'm a demon and servant of my master, the Devil," it said.

"Wha – wha – what do you want with us?" stammered Chip.

"The question is, what do you want of my master?" Moloch replied.

We all looked at each other, mouths agape.

"We really didn't want anything, we were only having some fun," said Sam.

Moloch scratched his pointed chin with one of his talons. "Fun, eh!" it cried. "You dare to summon the forces of darkness and call it fun!" it stormed. Moloch then seemed to calm down. It sat and pondered the situation for a few moments.

"You did offer your souls to the Devil, didn't you?" Moloch asked.

I replied, "I suppose we did, but we didn't know what we were doing."

"It's just as well that I'm only his servant then," said Moloch. "You see, if this had been my master there would be no turning back. The contract would be sealed and he would have your souls," he added.

"You mean you're not going to harm us?" said Emma.

"Harm you? No. But I can help you," replied Moloch.

"What do you mean?" asked Emma.

"I'm just a minor demon, I don't have my Masters powers," explained Moloch. "But if you let me have your souls for a short while I can help you achieve all that you want to."

It then looked each of us square in the eye for a few moments, and continued. "Steve, you want to be a champion athlete, don't you? And Emma, you want to be up there on a cat-walk in Paris, don't you? I can put you in the movies, Sam, no problems. As for you, Chip, I can help you start your own computer company and make a success of it. Ben, dear boy, I can make you that great scientist you so want to be. All these things I can do," said Moloch.

"Our souls, for a short while?" asked Chip.

"Absolutely! You give them to me for a few years, I'll fulfil your ambitions and then return them to you," assured Moloch.

"How can we trust you?" I asked.

Moloch seemed irked that I had brought up the question of trust. "Trust, dear boy? It's me who is doing you the favour!" it cried. "If my Master knew what I was offering you all, I'd be in very deep trouble. I'm the one going out on a limb here!"

We looked at each other not sure what to do next. Was Moloch's offer too good to be true, and could we trust him? Could we just walk away from this scene and be good boys and girls and forget all about it?

We were all terrified and couldn't think straight. Nobody knew what to say or was too frightened to utter a word.

"How can we trust you?" I asked.

Moloch seemed irked that I had brought up the question of trust. "Trust, dear boy? It's me who is doing you the favour," it cried. "If my Master knew what I was offering you all, I'd be in very deep trouble. I'm the one going out on a limb here."

We looked at each other not sure what to do next. Was Moloch's offer too good to be true, and could we trust him? Could we just walk away from this scene and be good boys and girls and forget all about it?

We were all terrified and couldn't think straight. Nobody knew what to say or was too frightened to utter a word

Chapter 4

"Well, I'm waiting," said Moloch. "I may be consigned to Hell for eternity, but I don't have time to burn," he chortled to himself.

We were too stunned and terrified to appreciate the joke.

"My Master will start to wonder what I've been up to. Please, let me show what I can do for you," Moloch said.

There before us, against the rear wall of the church, was a vision of what the future could be like for us. Somehow, Moloch was projecting against the wall a film of the possible future.

We watched Steve as an athlete in his prime competing in the Olympic decathlon. He was running, jumping and throwing better than anyone ever before. Then was collecting a gold medal. He had made it.

Then Emma appeared walking down a catwalk at a fashion show in a designer gown. The music blared out and the audience screamed for more. The camera flash guns popped everywhere. Her face was on the cover of every fashion magazine. She was a success.

Next we were at the Oscars with all the movie stars. There stood Sam on the stage. She was receiving the Oscar for best actress. The crowd cheered and stamped their feet. There she was – best actress.

Chip appeared on the cover of *Computer Monthly*. The headline said "Rising Star". There were vast factories making his computers. Chip was shaking hands with royalty and politicians. He was admired.

Finally, there was a vision of myself in the future. I had developed a cure for the common cold. I was nominated for a Nobel Prize and had the respect and gratitude of millions of people. Was it within my grasp?

I knew deep down that each of us would do almost anything to achieve what Moloch had just shown us. But would we go as far as to sell our souls? I looked at my four companions and tried to gauge their reactions.

Steve had a wide smile on his face and looked ready to do the deal there and then. Emma appeared wide-eyed in wonderment at what she had just been shown. Was she for the deal as well? As for Chip, he looked as if his brain was working overtime trying to weigh up his options. Sam had stopped shaking with fear and was now biting her lower lip. She didn't seem that sure the deal was for her.

Could I get away with this? I wondered to myself. Was Moloch, the little demon, to be trusted? Yes, I deeply wanted the vision of success that Moloch had shown me. But, was it worth the price of my soul?

"Let me try and persuade you a little further," said Moloch. "I've shown you what I can do if you give me your souls for a while, and I'm sure you like what you see." After a short pause, to give us time to think, he continued, "However, if you don't give me what I want, I will make your lives hell!"

We all gasped at what Moloch had just said.

"If I cannot have your souls, then I shall do everything in my power to thwart your ambitions," said Moloch.

Sam cried, "No way, that's not fair!"

"You try to raise the forces of darkness, and then talk to me about fairness?" said Moloch loudly. He then gave out a demonic laugh to himself.

"But, we didn't understand what we were doing!" cried Chip.

Moloch replied, "Fairness and understanding are not qualities that my master deals in. You surely know that, don't you!"

"So, the deal is, you have our souls for a while and we get to fulfil our ambitions. Or else, you will make life tough for us," I said.

"Not just tough, dear Ben, I will ruin each of your lives," whispered Moloch with glee.

Steve jumped in and said, "Okay, I'll do it!"

I thought the vision of success would be too much for him to resist. He was always too eager to succeed.

"Ah, we have some leadership being shown by Steve," Moloch pointed out.

"I'll do it too," added Emma. It was typical of her to agree with Steve so readily.

I looked at Chip and Sam and couldn't believe the other two had agreed so quickly. Were they so ambitious that nothing else mattered?

Chip gulped and said, "Count me in. I want to be somebody."

"I'd rather be a winner than a loser!" said Sam. She respected Chip's intelligence and this probably made her agree to the deal.

"Now that just leaves you, Ben," Moloch said. "How about it? Your companions are all for the deal."

My head was spinning as I looked at them all. They had all agreed to sell their souls! Was it really such a terrible thing to do? Of course it was! But I so badly wanted to be one of them.

"Well?" inquired Moloch.

"Yea, okay," I blurted out. My heart sank as I instantly regretted what I had just said.

"Good! I'm sure you've all made the right decision," Moloch cried with delight. "Leave it to me and all your dreams will come true."

"When do we get our souls back?" I questioned Moloch.

He gave me a little grin and said, "Don't worry."

The eerie red light that he had been bathed

in disappeared and left us in complete darkness.

"Moloch, are you still here?" Steve cried out into the darkness.

There was no reply. He had gone.

Chip began lighting the candles again to let us see each other clearly. We were all too stunned to talk for a while. Breaking the silence, Sam said, "Did all that really just happen?"

From my expression and those of the others, she was left in no doubt that we had just had a visit from a demon called Moloch. We had just sold our souls!

Chapter 5

We left the church in a hurry. I suppose we were desperate to reach a safe public place where there was lots of light and people. There was little conversation as we all must have been considering what we had just done. The cinema down the road was just emptying so we mingled with the crowd for a while.

"I feel safer now, I'd better be heading home," said Emma.

"Me too," added Sam.

"Okay, I'll see you home," said Steve.

They strode off into the night without even saying goodbye to Chip and myself. Chip looked at me and nodded in the direction of our way home. We walked at a very brisk pace with an uneasy feeling. Each of us kept looking behind our back every few seconds as if expecting to be chased by the Devil himself.

I reached my driveway and said, "See you tomorrow. Safe home!" Chip gave a nod and set off home, which was just around the corner from mine.

I turned the key and felt very relieved to be back in my home with my family. Dad came into the hallway and remarked, "Where have you been? You look as if you've seen a ghost!"

With a half-hearted smile I replied, "It's just very cold out tonight," and shrugged my shoulders. "I think I'll go to bed," I explained. I wished Mum and Dad goodnight and went upstairs.

By midnight the house was silent with everyone in bed. My mind was replaying the events of the evening again and again. The bedside light remained on as I had no wish to be plunged into darkness and the terrors that it now held. I tried to think of other things but it was impossible.

I awoke with a shudder. I must have drifted off and one of my parents had came in and put the light off. Looking around my room I suddenly gasped. There again was the mysterious red light. Moloch was standing at the bottom of my bed. I closed my eyes and hoped I was dreaming. After a few seconds I squinted one eye open. Moloch was still there.

"Yes, I'm here," he said.

I pulled the bed covers up to my chin and said, "Go away!"

Moloch replied, "But I'm here to help you. We have a deal. I thought I'd pay you a visit to explain things a bit better."

"Please, go away!" I pleaded.

"Oh, come on! I'm not here to harm you," said Moloch. After he said this I relaxed a little.

"Don't worry, your parents won't hear anything. Not unless you want them to," whispered Moloch.

CRASH!

The contents of the bookshelf then flew to the floor with an almighty clatter. A bedroom door opened and bare feet padded along the hallway towards my room. The door opened and my dad peered in.

"What do you think you're doing at this time of night!" stormed dad.

"It wasn't me, the books just fell off," I replied.

"All by themselves?" asked dad. I nodded vigorously after noticing that Moloch was nowhere to be seen.

"We'll have words in the morning, now get to sleep!" dad ordered.

As the door closed behind him, Moloch reappeared at the bottom of the bed.

"What did you do that for?" I questioned.

"Just to show you what a little devil I can be," said Moloch. "You see, dear Ben, this is serious business. I have your soul, but you have a very bright future."

Then, as quickly as he had appeared he was gone again. I quietly called his name a few times, but Moloch did not return. The rest of the night I hardly slept at all with the added worry that I would now have to face the anger of my dad in the morning.

After washing and dressing, I crept down the stairs hoping to avoid dad before he went to work. I was expecting the worst as I walked into the kitchen and found him finishing his breakfast. He smiled at me and then returned to looking at his morning paper. Sitting opposite him at the table I found his silence about last night very awkward. I eventually plucked the courage and decided to try and apologise.

"About last night, dad," I started.

"Oh, not to worry, Ben. Let's just forget about it," he interrupted. With that he stood up, kissed mum, and went off to work.

I sat there amazed at how I'd been let off so

lightly. Then I thought to myself "Could this be due to Moloch? Was the demon able to influence the feelings and thoughts of those around me?"

The events over the breakfast table had cheered me as I walked to school. Steve stood at the school gates waiting for me with Emma and Sam. Steve grinned and said, "Welcome, brother. Did you get a visit last night as well?"

"Yes! Do you mean you did too?" I enquired.

"It seems we all had a visit from Moloch last night," said Emma.

Chip then appeared and looked a bit agitated. He whispered, "You'll never guess what happened last night."

We looked at him with wry smiles across our faces. Chip quickly realised it had happened to us all. We walked through the school gates and wondered how school life would be with Moloch helping to smooth the way.

Chapter 6

In another part of town, Moloch had just finished doing another deal for some more souls. He was feeling quite pleased with himself. Then, in a flash of fire and brimstone, his Master appeared before him. The Devil himself had come to question Moloch about his recent activities.

The Devil loomed towards Moloch and boomed out, "Moloch, what have you been up to?"

"Just the usual, Master. Collecting souls for

you," Moloch replied.

"And what of those school kids the other night?" inquired the Devil.

"Which ones would that be, Master?" said Moloch.

Flames sprang up around the Devil as Moloch tried his patience. "You know who I mean – Ben, Steve, Sam, Emma and Chip."

Moloch, with head bowed, realised he had been caught out and said slowly, "Ah, those kids, Master."

This was not the first time that Moloch had been doing deals for himself behind his Master's back. A few times he had sought the opportunity of gaining a few souls for himself. The promise of only borrowing them for a short time was a con. The selling of souls was a one-way contract. They could never be returned. Those who had sold their souls to Moloch were helped to fulfil the ambitions they had. Most were happy with the bargain they had struck. That was – until they died.

Moloch liked to collect souls just as his Master did, and enjoyed the challenge of getting people to sell their souls to him. Secretly, Moloch revelled in the idea that he could keep his own collection of souls a secret from his Master. The Devil, however, did not agree with this way of doing business. All souls collected by Moloch and other demons were to be for the Devil alone.

"Moloch, you have disappointed me," said the Devil. "Now, I'll have to find these kids and tell them the real situation."

"Do you have to, Master? It's only five young souls!" pleaded Moloch.

"Yes, there can never be any exceptions.

They must be mine," answered the Devil.

Moloch then told the Devil who the kids were and where to find them. The little demon explained how they all burned with ambitions, and they had shown they were willing to do anything to fulfil them. Trying to explain his disobedience, Moloch told the Devil it had been too good an opportunity to miss. Five young souls captured that easily was too much of a temptation.

The Devil accepted that the temptation for Moloch had been too much. After all, falling to temptation was what being a demon was all about. If Moloch had been honest all along then the Devil would really have been worried.

"I'll confront them tonight," said the Devil. "Now, get out of my sight!"

Chapter 7

During the school day, which had gone very smoothly for all of us, we arranged to meet up in the evening to discuss the events of the last twenty-four hours. Not wanting to tempt fate, we had avoided the suggestion of meeting up in the old church again. Instead, the venue was to be the calm and safety of Chip's house.

Chip showed us through the door and up to his spacious bedroom. The room was, of course, covered with computing stuff. "Take a seat, if you can find one," said Chip.

"I can't believe how nice Brownly was to-day," began Sam. Mr Brownly was our English teacher and was not noted for his good humour. In fact he seemed to specialise in making most pupils' lives a misery.

"Yea, do you think this demon stuff is really working?" asked Chip.

"Maybe it's too early to tell," I replied.

"I think the signs look good for all of us," added Steve.

We then went over the events of last night. After a couple of hours, when it reached about nine o'clock, we had talked the happenings of last night over and over again. "Let's go get some burgers and fries," said Steve.

We filed out of Chip's house into the night. When we reached the bottom of the road we turned right and were confronted by a strange bank of fog further up the street. Then, silently out of the fog, a huge black limousine appeared and glided towards us. The car stopped beside us. I tried to peer inside, but the windows were blacked out.

Suddenly, a door slowly opened. A mist fell from the car floor onto the road and drifted away.

"Come inside!" ordered a deep voice.

Although I suspect we all wanted to run away, we were drawn to the car by some powerful force. We could not resist the order to enter from the occupant of the car.

The car was huge, so there was plenty of room for us to gather around the occupant in the back seats. Inside sat a tall handsome man in a black suit. The car was quite gloomy and the occupant's features were not easily seen. He appeared to have very dark hair and a strong angular face. Everything about him gave the impression of immense power.

"I think you all know who I am," stated the figure.

I certainly did, and I think my companions did too. We looked at each other not knowing what to say. After a moments silence Chip spoke up.

"Are you," Chip paused, he took a gulp and finished "the Devil?"

"Yes, and we have some business to attend to," replied the Devil.

"I'll come straight to the point," he continued. "I'm afraid you have all been duped by my servant, Moloch." We listened in shock.

"You cannot sell your souls for only a short

while and expect to get them back. Moloch lied! You made a deal with a demon acting on my behalf and you were misled," explained the Devil.

Our eyes widened in terror as we dreaded what the Devil was going to say next.

"Do you mean the deal is off then?" asked Sam, hopefully.

"Oh no. A deal is deal. Your souls are mine forever!" said the Devil.

We gasped. Emma put her head in her hands and Chip let out a long sigh. I sat thinking what a fool I had been in the first place to agree a deal with Moloch. Why did I allow greed and ambition to cloud my judgement?

"Look on the bright side," the Devil said with an evil smile on his face. "All that Moloch promised you, I will fulfil. Your ambitions will be met in full. The future is there for the taking!"

Suddenly, Sam, who was close to tears shouted, "No! Never! Never! Never!"

The Devil looked taken aback by this outburst.

Just as he tried to speak again, Sam interrupted, "You are evil, horrible and you cheated. The deal is off!"

"Yea, it's all off. You can't have my soul forever!" added Chip.

"But you agreed to sell your souls," reasoned the Devil.

"Not to you, and not forever!" I replied instantly.

The Devil paused for a moment and then said, "Whether you promised your souls to Moloch or me does not matter. It's the principle of the deal that counts."

"No chance! You can keep your deal! We

deny you our souls!" said Steve with real purpose in his voice. "We'll succeed in life without any help from you!"

The Devil now looked annoyed and said, "I hope you know the consequences of your actions," said the Devil.

"What do you mean?" I asked.

"I am not to be messed around with. I will have my way or else!" the Devil said threateningly.

"You can't have our souls – no way!" I cried.

"Just get out then, you stupid kids!" ordered the Devil.

We climbed over each other in our rush to get out of the car. The car then glided off as silently as it had arrived into a bank of fog and disappeared.

"Hey, do you think we're free from him?" inquired Sam.

"Maybe," Chip replied.

I had my doubts that we had seen the last of the Devil. What did the Devil mean when he had said, "...or else!"

Chapter 8

We met up in school the next morning. Chip suggested we go into an empty classroom for a private conversation between the five of us. All of us looked very tired and I guessed none of us had slept very much.

"Did you have any visitors last night, Ben?" Steve asked me.

"No, a peaceful night," I replied.

"Good, it appears all of us had a peaceful night then," Emma said.

Each of us breathed a sigh of relief and seemed to relax.

"Maybe we are in the clear," said Chip.

BANG!

We almost jumped out of our skins. The door which we had closed behind us flew open and crashed against the wall.

After a moment, Steve went to the doorway and looked into the corridor. We could hear laughter and footsteps running away.

"It's that Roberts kid!" said Steve. "I'll wring his neck when I catch up with him."

"He's always up to mischief," said Emma.

I gulped and commented, "For a moment I thought it was the Devil himself trying to frighten us."

"Yea, that's what I thought too," said Emma.

Steve grinned and said, "At least we have an explanation for that scary event."

Chip was flicking through a book he had brought to school with him. It was a very old looking, leather bound, black book. He found the page he was looking for and began muttering to himself.

"What are you up to, Chip?" I enquired.

"Trying to ensure we get out of this mess," he replied. "This is where I found the chant that we used for your initiation the other night."

The book was an old volume that Chip had found in a second-hand book shop. It was all about the occult and witchcraft.

Chip explained, "I only picked it up for a laugh. I never dreamed the chant would actually work."

Chip probably thought it was a great idea

at the time. He always liked to show everybody how intelligent he was. But this time it had backfired badly. The problem for Chip now was to show us how bright he was – and get us out of trouble.

"Is there anything in there that we can try to reverse what we've done?" I asked.

"That's just what I'm looking for," answered Chip.

Chip scoured the book for a few minutes and then announced, "There is something here that might do the trick."

He passed the book to me and pointed out the section in question. The book was very fragile and smelt stale. I looked at the pages which was full of Latin text – which I didn't understand. It explained that a ceremony with a bible and salt could be used to banish evil spirits.

"That's why we throw salt over our shoulders – for good luck," Chip explained.

"Huh?" I didn't understand.

"We throw salt over our shoulders to ward off the Devil," said Chip.

"Hey, this sounds like we're getting somewhere now!" Steve said.

"Right, shall we do it tonight then?" asked Emma.

Steve looked unhappy and said, "I've a lot on."

He was in serious training for the national school trials in athletics. His training schedule was very strict and he hated it being changed. Steve was determined to pave the way for a successful career in athletics and knew he had to be dedicated. It seemed to me that nothing, not even our souls, would stop him from trying to achieve his goal. How could he be so selfish and stubborn?

"We'll do it soon though, okay," he added.

I was angry with his excuse, but the others went along with his decision. They always seemed to agree with him.

"Look! This is a pretty major problem we have here!" I said. "I think we should try to settle it as soon as possible."

"Another day or two won't make any difference," said Steve.

"Yea. I have loads of project work to do as well," added Chip.

"And I've to organise a fashion show too," said Emma.

I turned to Sam for a response. She looked at Steve, Chip and Emma, and said, "I'm with them. Another day won't matter."

I realised I could not persuade them other-wise. I sighed and said, "Okay."

We filed out of the classroom. I was last to leave. As I went to close the door behind me, a strong gust of wind blew books and papers all around the room.

"Hey, look!" I cried.

They looked at the mess inside. Steve shrugged his shoulders.

"It was only the wind – don't get jumpy," he said.

"But where did that gust come from?" I asked.

Chip tried to give it a scientific explanation, "The air circulating in the corridors sometimes sucks the air from a classroom – it seems like the wind."

"That's right," said Emma. "There is sometimes a strong breeze blowing down these corridors."

"But maybe it was the Devil trying to frighten us!" I exclaimed.

"You worry too much," replied Steve confidently.

"Yea, cool down or you'll have us all on edge," said Sam.

Considering we had been talking to the Devil and Moloch I thought we had plenty to be on edge about. As usual, they were so cool and confident with the situation we were in. That's what I liked about them. It was that appearance that attracted me to them – and had caused this problem with the Devil.

Chapter 9

Two days later and it was Steve's big day . He had made it into the trials for the national championships. He really fancied himself as the ultimate athlete, and with good reason. Nobody could touch him when it came to athletics. Although he considered himself an all-rounder, the pole vault was his best event.

The trials were being held at our school track and we decided we were duty bound to cheer on one of our elite. Just about everyone else in the school had decided to cheer Steve on as well. There was a huge crowd to take in the afternoon's events. The crowd and atmosphere was no problem to Steve, he loved it.

He was limbering up under the instruction of Mr Jarvis, the coach, when the four of us approached him to pass on our support. Mr Jarvis then slipped away to take care of other athletes under his instruction. "I'll be back in a moment," said Mr Jarvis as he disappeared into the crowd.

"You can do it!" encouraged Emma.

"Of course I can," replied the super-confidant Steve.

I was amazed how the recent events concerning Devils and souls had allowed him to concentrate on his athletics. But, Steve was special. We all were sure that he would do well if not win the national championship itself.

The pole vault competition was about to begin and Mr Jarvis had not reappeared.

"I don't need his advice anyway," remarked Steve.

"Yea, go for it man!" I cried.

Steve took a few deep breaths and stared down the runway towards the bar. He took off, built up speed and then vaulted over the bar with ease.

He did not have it all his own way though, and the competition was fierce. After five rounds of the event Steve was being pressed very hard by another boy. People were saying this boy was a dark horse and he had improved in every round. Some were even saying that he was going to beat Steve.

It was the last round and Steve was limbering up for his final vault. He knew that this vault had to be special – his best ever. If it went to plan he would even break the record for his age group. This was what Steve really wanted. A record vault would set him on the road to glory and a great career in athletics.

The crowd parted around Steve, and Mr Jarvis appeared again. He was carrying a pole and presented it to Steve.

"Here, try this son," said Mr Jarvis. "It's a special pole I had made for you. It could be the difference between winning and losing."

"Why would I want to change poles now?" inquired Steve.

"It's a special plastic, Steve. It's got bend and spring like you've never seen before," replied Mr Jarvis.

Steve grabbed it and stood at the end of the runway looking mean. He took some huge breaths, stared coldly at his competition, and charged down the runway.

With huge strides he built up tremendous speed. He threw himself into the vault with all his might. The pole bent to an incredible angle and began to spring straight again propelling Steve upwards.

CRACK! The pole snapped. Steve was in mid-air and had a look of horror on his face for a second. He then fell back on the half of the pole which was still planted in the ground. It went straight through him with a sickening slurp. He hung there dead – impaled on the pole that Mr Jarvis had given him.

There were screams of horror and Emma buried her face into my chest. Teachers and officials rushed to Steve's body. All except for Mr Jarvis, where was he?

I hadn't noticed him since he gave the special pole to Steve. Why was he not around? If it hadn't been for his stupid new pole this would never have happened.

Steve's body was laid on the ground and covered with a coat. Mr Jarvis then came running up and screamed, "What's happened?"

"It's all your fault. You and your stupid pole!" screamed Emma.

"What pole?" asked Mr Jarvis.

"That special one you gave him for the final round," I replied.

Puzzled, Mr Jarvis said, "I never gave him any pole. I've been on the phone for the last ten minutes. How could I be here to give him a pole?"

I looked at Emma and said, "This is terrible – what a freak accident to happen to him."

Emma sobbed to me, "I don't think it was any accident."

"Do you mean the Devil had a hand in Steve's death?" said Sam.

"It makes sense, maybe the Devil is out for revenge because we denied him our souls," I replied.

Chapter 10

The following day we met outside Sam's house in the morning and went to the park. We had a lot to discuss. Sam and Emma sat on a bench whilst Chip and myself paced around them.

"It could just have been an accident," I stated to them.

"Maybe. It seems like more than coincidence to me though," said Chip.

Emma sobbed quietly, and was comforted by Sam putting her arm around her. Holding back her tears, Emma said, "What happened with Mr Jarvis?"

"The police checked out his story and it seemed he was on the phone all the time," Chip replied.

"So the Mr Jarvis we all saw was not him at all?" said Sam.

"It would seem that way. Someone, or something, was impersonating Mr Jarvis," Chip said.

I didn't want to think about who was responsible. A shiver went down my spine as I recalled the sight of Steve being impaled on the broken pole. The look of terror on his face as he realised what was about to happen will haunt me forever.

Sam asked, "What did the police say about the pole."

"I heard that they had taken it away to be investigated. They suspect that it may have been tampered with," I answered.

Emma spoke through her tears, "It must have been the work of the Devil. Who else would want to see Steve die in such a horrible way."

"Yea. Why would someone want to impersonate Jarvis?" asked Sam.

Chip looked at me, but neither of us could give an answer to Sam's question. The thought that the Devil had killed Steve in such a horrible way filled me with dread. Would the Devil strike again?

CROAK!

The loud noise made us jump. A huge black crow was in the tree just beside the bench. It was so large that it seemed strange we hadn't noticed as we sat at the bench. I looked up at the large dark ugly figure on the branch. It looked straight back at me with its beady black eyes.

CROAK! CROAK! CROAK!

The crow almost seemed to be baiting us. Was it more than just an old crow sitting in a tree? Could it be laughing at us and what had happened to Steve? I reached down to pick up a small branch to throw at the beast. Before I could take aim it had spread its great black wings and swooped towards us.

It just missed Chip's head as we ducked and scattered away from the tree. It swooped on us twice more and then flapped off into the distance.

"That crows gone mad!" cried Chip as he watched it fly away. "What did we do to provoke it?"

"Who knows!" I replied.

"I don't think that was any ordinary crow!" cried Emma. "Let's get out of here!"

We ran out of the park looking for the safety of indoors. We found a small café which was deserted.

The owner was behind the counter and said, "What's up with you lot?"

We were all gasping for breath, and Sam replied rudely "Nothing!"

"You look as if you've been chased by the devil himself," he chortled.

Emma yelled back at him, "It's none of your business!"

"Only asking, there's no need to bite my head off," said the owner.

Emma glared at him angrily, and I was a bit embarrassed by her actions.

The owner spoke again, "If you're going to take that attitude, young lady, you can leave right now!"

I tried to calm the situation by replying, "Sorry, she's just upset. We've had a fright that's all."

"No trouble I hope," said the owner. "I don't want any trouble in here."

"Nothing to worry about," I reassured the owner. "Can we have four coffees, please?"

The owner smiled and said, "That's better, four coffees coming up."

A minute later he placed the coffees on our table. We had calmed down enough to try and figure out what had happened in the park.

"It could be just coincidence," Chip reasoned.

Emma whispered so the owner could not

hear, "First, Steve dying and now that crow in the park. I think it's the work of the Devil."

"Are you serious?" asked Sam.

"Deadly!" replied Emma in an ominous tone.

Chapter 11

A few days had passed and we were beginning to get over Steve's death. There had been no more strange happenings or visitations. We still had to fix a date for using the ceremony Chip found in his book to see off the Devil. This still annoyed me, but as nothing else horrible had happened to us it did not seem so urgent.

Emma, especially, had perked up because she was organising and appearing in a fashion show to raise funds for charity. It was good to see her forget about Steve for a while and concentrate on something that she really loved.

The show was to begin at seven o'clock and was being held in the school hall. Emma was running around making sure that everything was going to be perfect. The rest of us were on hand to help with any odd jobs that arose. I was making sure that the carpet on the catwalk was as smooth as possible. Jones, the school janitor, was giving me a hand.

"We don't want any bumps or dips in the carpet," said Jim. I gave a nod and a smile as he stated the obvious.

"Yea, it could be dangerous up there," I agreed.

We smoothed the carpet as best we could but we came to a section that was giving us a problem. The catwalk was made from sections of scaffolding, like the ones that painters and deco-rators use. On top was chip board to form a flat surface to lay the carpet upon. The whole thing was about two metres high and stretched out from the stage for about twenty metres. Our school hall was so big that the catwalk had to be this size to do the show justice.

The problem arose in the middle section where parts of the scaffolding didn't quite join properly. This left a gap just large enough to get a heel trapped in. Jones and I tried our best but we couldn't get the gap to close up.

"Emma, we've got a problem," I explained.

"What now!" she snapped back.

I was annoyed by her tone and said, "If you don't want my help then I'll go."

She sighed and said, "I'm sorry, Ben, there's just so much to do that I'm frantic."

"I understand," I replied. "There's a tiny gap in the middle section that we haven't got time to fix properly," I continued.

"That's okay, Ben, I'll warn everybody about it. Now I must get on. See you later!" she cried and rushed off.

The show was about to begin. Music filled the room and the lights were dimmed. Chip and myself were backstage helping to work the spotlights. The announcer said, "Ladies and Gentlemen, here is a collection brought to you by Emma Maine."

Emma burst onto the catwalk looking very elegant. She had a huge smile on her face and was obviously loving every minute of it. The audience gave her rapturous applause. She moved down the catwalk, turned at the bottom and returned to the stage behind the curtain. I saw her raise her hands in the air and shout a silent, "Yes!" She must have been relieved and proud that the show was off the ground and moving.

Model after model paraded up and down the catwalk. After a while I began to get concerned about the gap in the middle section. It appeared to be getting bigger and I thought it was only going to get worse unless something was done about it.

Emma had just came through the curtain again and I approached her, "Emma, it's the catwalk," I said.

"Oh shut up, Ben, don't worry," she replied and rushed off again for another change.

I looked around to try and find Jones to see what he thought. He was nowhere to be seen. Where had he gone, I thought to myself. Then I got a tap on the shoulder. I turned round and there was Jones.

"What about that gap then, Ben?" he said.

"Yea, I'm a bit concerned about it," I said.

"Tell you what. I'll climb along under the catwalk so as not to disturb the show, and see what I can do to fix it," Jones explained.

Jones then gathered some tools together and went under the curtain next to the stage.

The show was nearing its big finale and Emma was ready for her moment in the spotlight. Her last costume was a shimmering gown and she looked fabulous. She composed herself, gave Chip and me a huge smile and strode onto the catwalk. I watched her glide along the catwalk, wondering how proud she must have felt. To great applause, she turned and made her way back along the catwalk.

I suddenly gasped. I was sure I saw a

movement in the middle of the catwalk where the gap was. Emma strode closer and closer and I watched in horror as her heel seemed to get trapped in the gap and she lost her balance. The look on her face seemed to suggest that she was going to fall and it was going to be awful. In a split second she had toppled over the catwalk and there was a terrible dull thud as she landed head first on the floor below.

After a moments silence there where screams of horror from the crowd. Chip and I rushed to the scene. A woman from the audience, who must have been a doctor, said, "I'm afraid she's dead. She must have fractured her skull."

What had Jones done?

I looked under the catwalk to see where he was, but he was nowhere to be seen. Had he ran off when the terrible event occurred?

I looked at Chip in disbelief. Another of our elite band had died, in what appeared to be, a freak accident.

"Who's next?" asked Chip.

Chapter 12

The remaining three of us stood outside the school after the terrible event of Emma's death. We were all shocked and Sam was still sobbing. I put my arm around her to comfort her.

"I tell you, Jones told me he was going to try and fix the gap, and then he went under the catwalk," I explained to Sam and Chip.

"But people have said that Jones was nowhere near the catwalk when she fell," said Chip. "He was at the back of the hall with some of the teachers discussing who was going to be doing the clearing up."

"It's just like what happened to Steve with Mr Jarvis – except that it wasn't Mr Jarvis," said Sam.

"Yes, I think the Devil is impersonating people we trust to bring about our deaths, and then he can collect our souls!" I exclaimed.

"What will we do?" asked Sam.

"We'll need to raise the Devil again and see if we can get him to stop," replied Chip.

"I don't know about that," said Sam.

"We don't appear to have much choice," I said.

"Right then. We'll go back to the old church now and see what can be done," Chip said.

We nodded in agreement and set off for the old church. We took a detour to Chip's house to collect the black book which had the ceremony in it. He emerged after a couple of minutes.

"Okay. Let's do it," he forcefully announced.

"Salt!" said Sam.

"Salt?" puzzled Chip.

Then he remembered that salt was needed for the ceremony. Running back inside the house he quickly got the salt.

"I need it for an experiment," he explained to his mother as he flew out the door.

I was full of fear when we approached the rear of the church. We clambered through the window and looked around inside. The candles were still there from our original visit. Chip had some matches and began to light them again.

"Can you remember that Latin mumbo-jumbo?" I asked Chip.

"Sure, it's hard not to forget after causing

all this mayhem!" he replied.

The robes we had used for the fake ceremony were still lying around also, and we put them on. Chip poured the salt in a circle and opened his book.

He began to chant the Latin phrases that were used for my initiation. We waited to see what happened.

Silence.

After a few minutes, which seemed like an age, I turned to Chip and said, "Try it again, its our only chance." Chip took a deep breath and repeated the chanting again. We waited.

Nothing.

"One last try, now all concentrate," said Sam.

Chip chanted the weird Latin phrases again and then stopped. The mysterious red light appeared again and there stood Moloch.

"You summon me again – for what reason?" said Moloch.

"We want to see the Devil, not you. You lied to us," said Chip.

"We want to know why the Devil has killed our friends?" I said.

"I'd have thought that was obvious. You tried to reject the deal we had made, and this upset my master," Moloch replied.

"Are we all to die?" asked Sam.

Moloch laughed and said, "All mortals must die, its just a matter of time."

"I didn't mean that," Sam pleaded. "Are we to die so young in such horrible ways?"

"That I cannot answer. It is up to my master," said Moloch. "He may be satisfied with taking two of you, but then again, he may not."

"Where does that leave us then?" I asked.

"My Master has done this sort of thing before. He likes to set an example. You may be OK , but I can't say for sure," replied Moloch.

"Why should we believe you!" cried an angered Sam.

"You have no choice," said Moloch through a wide grin.

Chip then picked up the salt container and threw it at the demon.

"Be gone foul spirit and leave us in peace!" he shouted.

There was a horrible shriek and a blast of wind blowing out all the candles. Moloch was gone.

"That sorted him!" cried Chip.

I breathed a sigh of relief and turned to Chip. There in his hands I saw the old book beginning to smoulder.

I gasped and shouted, "Chip, watch out –
the book!"

Chip reacted immediately by dropping the
book at his feet. It lay there smoking for a few
seconds and then burst into flames. For such a
small book there was a huge amount of smoke
being given off. We looked on in horror as an image began to appear in the smoke. It was the
Devil. He smiled and then gave out the most evil
laughter I've ever heard. It shook me to the core.

Thankfully, Chip still had his wits about
him. Managing to break free from his terror, he
grabbed a handful of salt and threw it at the image of the Devil. In a second the image was gone.
The smoke, flames and, oddly, any remains of
the book had also disappeared. We were left in
total darkness and silence.

"Well done, Chip – you saved us there," I said with gratitude.

"Yea, I think we got rid of him," he replied shaking with fear.

Chapter 13

The next morning we met up on our way to school. Sam and Chip said they'd had quiet nights – much the same as myself. We were all very relieved not to have had any more trouble from the Devil or Moloch. Although by the looks of us, none of us had any sleep at all.

"Do you think we'll be alright?" inquired Emma.

"Who knows," replied Chip with a sigh.

I tried to be positive and said, "Well, whatever happens we'll just have to get on with it."

"Yea, it's all so simple isn't it!" cried Sam. "We just hang around until we get lured to some gruesome end."

"Sam, try to relax," I pleaded.

Sam was sobbing and said, "If it wasn't for you we would never be in this mess."

"What do you mean!" I cried.

"We should never have bothered to dream up that crazy initiation ceremony for you," she said.

"How can that be my fault?" I queried.

Chip interrupted, "Stop it you two! This is bad enough without the three of us fighting each other."

Sam and I glared at each other.

"As Ben said, all we can do is try to get on with our lives," said Chip. "Hope for the best," he added with a smile.

We went through the school gates and to our classes.

Chip was working on a computer project. From the laboratory where I was, I could see across to the other wing of the school and the classroom where Chip was working at his computer. He was alone in the room and in conversation with Mrs Charles, the computing science teacher. She appeared to hand him a disk.

"Ben! Come away from the window and get on with your work," ordered Mr Andrews, my biology teacher.

I was concentrating on what I was doing for a while when I looked over to where Chip was. He seemed transfixed to the computer screen. Suddenly, I saw something move beside him.

I couldn't make it out at first, but it seemed to be a cable of some sort. Why would a cable be moving around? Then I realised what it was. I could see that it was the cable attached to the computer mouse. Why hadn't he seen what was happening?

Chip just stared into the screen as the cable was in mid-air next to him. To my horror the cable then began to wind around Chip's neck without him noticing. I was dumb struck. Chip's neck was wrenched backwards as the cable tightened round his neck. His hands were at his throat as he tried to struggle with the cable.

"Ben, what are you doing?" asked Mr Andrews. I stared on and couldn't answer him.

"Ben, answer me!" shouted the teacher.

I ran from the room to try and save Chip.

"Come back here, Ben. What on earth are

you doing?" shouted Mr Andrews.

"It's Chip," I cried. "I've got to save him."

My lungs were bursting by the time I got to the room where Chip was. I held my head when I saw Chip. He was lying slumped over the desk where he was working. The computer mouse cable hung from the desk onto the floor.

After a few moments, maybe minutes, my teacher came into the room. "My goodess, Ben, what's happened?" cried Mr Andrews. He checked Chip's pulse. He shook his head.

"Did you see what happened, Ben?" asked Mr Andrews.

"I saw something..." I replied.

"Go on," implored Mr Andrews.

"It was the mouse cable," I said. "He was strangled by the cable."

"But who did it, Ben?" asked Mr Andrews.

"Nobody," I replied. "The cable did it itself."

"What nonsense! Who did it, Ben?" cried Mr Andrews.

Mrs Jones came into the room and screamed when she saw the body of Chip.

She said, "I didn't know Chip was in here working alone."

"But I saw you talking to him and give him a disk," I insisted.

Mrs Jones replied, "No I didn't! I've been teaching a class for the last hour."

Then I realised that the Devil had impersonated Mrs Jones. The disk Chip was given was so interesting to him that he hadn't noticed what was really happening.

Mr Andrews grabbed me and shook me.

"Was it you?" he asked. I didn't answer.

"Right, you stay here and I'll go and get some help," said Mr Andrews as he left the room and locked the door behind him.

I looked at poor Chip and then immediately thought about Sam. Was she okay? Was Sam safe? Mrs Jones had been left to watch me, but I reckoned I could escape her. The room was on the ground floor, so I opened the window and jumped out into the school yard.

Chapter 14

I knew that Sam would be working on her video project in a classroom at the other side of the school. I bolted round the school and reached the room where Sam was working.

I banged on the window and shouted, "It's Chip!"

Sam looked confused and beckoned me to come into the classroom. As I ran around to the rear entrance I could see Mr Andrews and others looking for me in the school grounds.

I reached the corridor where Sam's room was. She was filming a report and using some spotlights suspended from the ceiling to provide a professional feel to the piece. As I ran down the corridor I wondered what I was going to say...

SNAP!

I couldn't believe what I was seeing. Sam looked up in horror as one of the spotlights directly above her fell and crashed onto her head. She didn't stand a chance.

"Sam!" I screamed and rushed to her side.

Blood poured from her, now, lifeless body. I held her hand, wishing she could come back to life.

The boy who was filming her said, "What did you do to that spotlight?"

"Me? I wasn't here," I replied.

"Yes, you were," he insisted. "I saw you

talking to Sam an hour ago and then getting ladders and adjusting that spotlight."

"It couldn't have been me. I was in the biology lab this morning," I explained.

"Yes, it was! Or have you an identical twin?" he said.

It then dawned on me; the Devil had been impersonating people again. In this case he had impersonated me and it had led to Sam's death.

Sam lay in front of me. She had been doing what she enjoyed – making videos. She thought I had been helping her, but instead the Devil was planning her death. I sat on the floor and cried.

Mr Andrews and two other teachers burst into the classroom.

"Grab him!" cried Mr Andrews.

"It wasn't me, don't you understand?" I said.

"We'll let the police decide that," he answered.

My arms were grabbed and pinned to my side.

The boy in the room said, "It was him. He must have rigged the light for it to fall."

The teachers looked at each other and nodded. I was taken away to the headmasters office and the police were called. They interviewed me about the deaths of Sam and Chip. I suppose to them my story must have seemed confused and silly. I just couldn't seem to get through to them that it was all the Devil's work.

I was led from the school, through an accusing and hostile crowd of kids, parents and teachers into a police car.

How could they think that I had killed them?

Chapter 15

The car brought me to the police station where I was questioned again and then placed in a cell. Sitting alone in the cell I wondered if my life could get any worse. I had great ambitions, like my dead companions, but now I was being accused of murder.

I heard a key go into the cell door lock and the door opened. An officer stood there and said, "Right, son, come with me."

"More questions?" I inquired.

The officer didn't reply and escorted me to the interview room. He opened the door and there was a sight to gladden my eyes. My mum and dad were sitting there with the lawyer.

"Oh, Dad!" I cried.

He gave me a big hug and said, "Everything's going to be alright. Just tell the truth."

"That's what I've been doing, Dad, but they won't believe me," I said.

Dad then introduced the lawyer.

"This is Nathan Maxwell, he is going to be your lawyer," he said.

"I'm here to help you," said Maxwell in a comforting tone. "It's best if you tell us the truth."

"But I have been!" I cried.

We then went through my story again and again. This time the police included the deaths of

Steve and Emma as well. It seemed that I was under grave suspicion of being involved in all four deaths. The problem was that the four people who could clear my name were now dead. Witnesses had given statements that I was at, or near, all four deaths.

"You were seen fixing the spotlight just before it fell on Sam," said the police officer.

"That wasn't me – it was someone impersonating me. The Devil!" I explained.

"You were seen beside Chip's body and ran away from the scene. Isn't that suspicious?" inquired the officer.

"I had to see Sam!" I squealed.

"To shut her up maybe?" continued the officer.

"NO! NO! NO! It was the Devil," I screamed at the top of my voice.

The policeman sighed as if in frustration. He banged the table and said, "You will have to stop this nonsense about the Devil. How can you expect us to believe that!"

"But it's true! The Devil was after all of us!" I cried.

Mum intervened and said, "Ben, it's about time you dropped this tale about the devil and told us all the truth."

"Do you mean that my own mother doesn't believe me?" I said in indignation.

"The truth, Ben. For your own sake!" pleaded my father.

I was dumb struck that now my own father didn't believe what I was saying.

"This is getting nowhere," announced the officer. "We'll have to call in the psychiatrist!"

"What!" I cried.

My dad and the lawyer nodded in agreement.

"I'll see you later, Ben," said dad as he left the room.

My mother left the room crying and said, "Oh, Ben, what have you done?"

The officer then took hold of my arm and led me back to the cell. The door slammed and was locked. There I was alone and being accused of murder. Now, they also thought I was mad! Was I?

I closed my eyes for a few seconds wishing that it was all a bad dream. Then a voice from out of nowhere said, "It is not a dream Ben."

Startled, I opened my eyes to gaze upon the figure we had all met in the car that night a few days ago. It was the Devil himself.

"This is a fine mess you are in now. Isn't

it?" said the Devil.

I screamed, "Help! Help! He's here!"

A moment later an officer opened the door. "What's up with you?" he asked.

"The Devil was here," I explained.

The officer sighed and said, "Where is he now then?"

"But he was here a second ago!" I cried.

"I know it's been a long day and you are frightened, but try to calm down and get some rest," said the officer. With that he closed the cell door and turned the key.

"Don't leave me, he'll come back to get me!" I pleaded.

I could hear the officers footsteps going up the corridor outside. He must have met another officer. I faintly heard him say, "That murderer kid has really flipped. He says he's been talking to the Devil."

The other officer said, "The psychiatrist will have to see him in the morning. Chances are he'll be put into a funny farm."

I turned around and there again stood the Devil.

"They are convinced you are a mad murderer," said the Devil.

"But I'm innocent!" I exclaimed.

"They don't think so," replied the Devil. "It could all be so different though, Ben."

I knew what the Devil meant. "If I sell my soul to you, I can walk away from all this mess," I said.

"Yes, Ben, all this will seem like a bad dream," said the Devil.

Here I was, faced with a terrible decision to make. Should I agree to sell my soul? as I had done with Moloch. I could be free.

The Devil waited a while for my answer.

"No! Never!" I said with conviction.

"Ben, you are a fool! But I will have your soul one day," cried the Devil and then disappeared in a flash.

Chapter 16

I sat up through the night and pondered my fate. My soul had been saved from the Devil, but there was a heavy price to pay. I would have to lose my freedom to thwart the Devil from having my soul.

The psychiatrist arrived in the morning and began to question me. He was exactly as I imagined he would be. Dressed in a crumpled tweed suit, with a beard and small spectacles, he was like someone from a bad television programme.

Mum and dad were there again and said, "Remember, Ben, tell the truth."

Anger rose within me when they said this. Why could they not bring themselves to believe their own son? Had the Devil turned them against me too?

"Hi, Ben, I'm Tom Barnet, a psychiatrist," he began. "I'm here to help you."

"You can start by believing me!" I cried.

"Ben, how long have you been having these visions?" he inquired with a sympathetic voice.

I sighed in frustration and said, "I am not mad. The Devil has killed my friends and has punished me for not selling my soul to him."

"So, the Devil made you kill your friends?" said Barnet.

"No, I had nothing to do with their deaths

– it was the Devil who disguised himself and killed them," I explained.

Barnet rose from his seat and paced around in front of me.

"Have you been having these meetings with the Devil for long?" he asked.

"No, it all began a few days ago," I replied.

He continued, "You were jealous of these people who died, weren't you?"

I felt he was trying to trap me into saying that had I envied them their confidence and success. Probably I did, but I did not kill them, and I had to try and convince him of this.

I explained, "I wanted to be part of their crowd – I liked them."

"Did they ever make you feel angry, Ben?" queried Barnet.

"Sometimes," I answered. "But not enough

to want to kill them!"

He sat down again and wrote some notes on a sheet of paper.

"I'm afraid you are very ill, Ben," he said. "We'll have to put you in a special hospital and give you some treatment."

"An asylum?" I asked.

Barnet paused for a moment and said, "Some would call it that. It's a place where people like you can be treated and kept safe."

"The Devil said this would happen," I stated.

Barnet put his arm on my shoulder and said, "Well, we want to stop the Devil saying these things to you – don't we."

Mum, dad and Barnet then had a conversation outside the room. After a few minutes they came back in.

Dad said, "They're going to take you away, Ben, to make you better. We will visit you when we can." He then hugged me and left the room.

"We want you to get better, son. At least it's better than going to jail," my mother said crying, and left.

I couldn't contain myself any longer and screamed, "Can't you see that I'm innocent? You are playing into his hands!"

"Ben, control yourself!" cried my mother from the corridor.

An officer grabbed me and said, "Yes, control yourself – we don't want to get hurt now, do we?"

I detected the loathing the officer had for me in his voice. Everyone was against me now. The Devil's plan for me had worked.

I was doomed!

Dad said, "They're going to take you away, Ben, to make you better. We will visit you when we can." He then hugged me and left the room.

"We want you to get better, son. At least it's better than going to jail," my mother said crying, and left.

I couldn't contain myself any longer and screamed, "Can't you see that I'm innocent? You are playing into his hands."

"Ben, control yourself," cried my mother from the corridor.

An officer grabbed me and said, "Yes, control yourself – we don't want to get hurt now, do we".

I detected the loathing the officer had for me in his voice. Everyone was against me and now The Devil's plan for me had worked.

I was doomed!

Chapter 17

Later that morning I was handcuffed and put into an ambulance. I was escorted by a policeman and what appeared to be a male nurse.

"Do you know what's happening?" asked the nurse.

"Yes. I'm going to the asylum," I replied with spite.

The nurse said, "It's called Moorville Special Hospital. We'll make you better."

It was worse than I had feared it would be.

I had my own cell – they called it a room. Four blank walls and a wash basin. If I wasn't mad when I came here, being in this cell was going to make me.

I observed the other patients around me. Some were walking around like zombies while others were scuttling about and screaming from time to time.

How could they possibly put me in here?

They must be violent and dangerous, I thought. I'll have to be constantly on my guard. But they probably thought the same of me, if they could think straight – which I doubted.

Would I ever be safe in here? I dreaded what the future would hold for me.

"When will I be allowed out of here?" I asked the doctor who came to examine me.

"I can't say, Ben – when you are better."

"Better?" I continued.

"When you face up to the truth," said the doctor.

"You mean when I admit that I murdered my friends!" I cried.

The doctor did not reply to my question.

He continued, "It will take some time for you to get better, Ben – maybe years."

My heart sank as he said these words.

After dark, I lay in my cell thinking about how terrible it had all turned out. Suddenly I was aware of a presence. There again stood the Devil.

"Are you ready to sell your soul yet, Ben," asked the Devil.

"No, never! Leave me alone," I replied.

The Devil laughed and said, "I'll keep coming back to see you until you are ready to deal."

My only comfort was, at least I had kept my soul from the clutches of the Devil. A horrible thought crossed my mind and sent a shiver down my spine.

How long will I be able to keep saying "No" to the Devil's deal?

We hope you have enjoyed this series of Shivers. In this series, there are six titles to collect.

This series was conceived by Edgar J. Hyde and much of the text was provided by his minions, under slavish conditions and pain of death! Thankfully, none of these minions defied their master and so we can say 'thank you' to them for toughing it out and making this series possible.

Edgar J. Hyde, however, has yet more plans for these dungeon-bound slaves. 'No rest for the wicked' is his motto!

Shivers

RAG & BONE MAN

In a small village the night after every funeral, an apparition of a Rag and Bone man, with his horse and cart, reputedly makes his way down the high street.

The trouble is, the person reporting the sight is normally the next person in a coffin!

Thus a conspiracy of silence prevails among the locals and the legend remains unconfirmed. Until that is, three cousins, after the death of an elderly relative, decide to investigate...

𝔖𝔥𝔦𝔳𝔢𝔯𝔰

PEN PALS

Two schoolgirl friends begin writing notes to each other for fun.

In time these notes start to contain suggestions that are not their own. Intrigued, they continue until it appears that two long lost sisters are using them to communicate with each other.

The story they tell reveals a need for revenge – and a need to fear someone the schoolgirls think of as a friend.

If only they knew which one...

Shivers

NOISY NEIGHBOURS

A seemingly puritanically-minded family move to a big run-down area in a big city.

They refuse to talk to their new neighbours as they regard them as inferior. But something doesn't quite fit with this family. At night all the wild, partying noises come from their house and through the blinds, the neighbours see shadows of what looks like inhuman forms.

Killjoys during the day – fun lovers at night, this Jekyll and Hyde type family come under the scrutiny of three teenage would-be ghost busters!

Shivers

PAYBACK TIME

A family's life is made a misery by loansharks who then discover that they have bitten off more than they can chew. The family pay back the moneylenders in carefully worked out instalments and with interest!

Mysteriously, the family is helped by the sympathetic previous tenant of their home, who was forced out by the same loansharks in the past

This tenant disappeared under unexplained circumstances and now seems to appear only at the moments of most need!

𝔖𝔥𝔦𝔳𝔢𝔯𝔰

COLD KISSER

All the boys at school want to kiss the new girl until one boy does. Word then gets around about her cold kiss which seemed to freeze him in time, like a temporary kiss of death.

Another boy, Tommy does all he can to resist kissing the new girl, Sally Anne.

Strangely, he feels as if he's known her before. But when and where?